The car reached the end of the st... ...ned into the main road. The Spuddy stood watching it until it disappeared and sensing the finality of his rejection made no whimper of entreaty or protest. After a few minutes he climbed to the top step of the empty house and lay down, staring along the street, his mixed tobacco eyes shadowed with the fatalistic acceptance of his plight. The neighbours lingered gossiping for a while before returning to their own homes. The street became quiet save for the mocking echoes of gull cries carried in by a sea wind. With a sigh the Spuddy's head sank down on to his outstretched paws but his eyes stayed wide and reflective, like those of a man meditating over future plans.

LILLIAN BECKWITH

The Spuddy

Decorations by Victor Ambrus

Arrow Books Limited
3 Fitzroy Square, London W1

An imprint of the Hutchinson Publishing Group

London Melbourne Sydney Auckland
Wellington Johannesburg and agencies
throughout the world

First published Hutchinson & Co (Publishers) Ltd 1974
Arrow edition 1976
Second impression 1977

Text and illustrations © Hutchinson & Co
(Publishers) Ltd 1974

Made and printed in Great Britain
by The Anchor Press Ltd
Tiptree, Essex

ISBN 0 09 913330 X

In memory of 'The Spuddy'

1

When Joe died Marie Glenn decided to say goodbye to her home in the brisk little fishing port of Gaymal and take herself off to begin a new life in Glasgow. All she was leaving behind was her husband's dog, 'the Spuddy', a thick set, grey-black mongrel which he had brought home as a puppy four years previously. He was called 'the Spuddy' simply because Joe had been in the habit of describing anyone who was, in his opinion, more than a little astute, as a 'Spuddy' and when the dog had begun to display a remarkable intelligence Joe had observed repeatedly, his voice full of admiration, 'He's a real Spuddy, that one'. So 'the Spuddy' he had become. Despite his hybridism (Joe used to say his coat looked as if someone had dipped him in a barrel of glue and then emptied a flock mattress over him) the dog had an air of aloof self-assurance emphasized by an arrogantly held head and a long droop of a setter-like tail which, as he moved with his easy sauntering gait, swung from side to side with the stateliness of an ermine cloak.

The bond between Joe and the Spuddy had never developed into devotion on either side for though he had housed him, licensed him and seen that he was well fed, Joe's feeling for the Spuddy was mostly approbation linked with an absent minded sort of affection while the Spuddy, accepting that he had an owner but not a master and too proud to beseech that which was not offered, retaliated by according to Joe the forbearing protectiveness he might have bestowed on a child.

Joe had worked as a fish porter down at the pier and thither the Spuddy had loyally accompanied him on six mornings of every week with such regularity that people said the dog ought to be drawing the same wages as the man. And certainly the Spuddy proved himself useful. If anything was dropped into the harbour and needed to be retrieved Joe had only to call the Spuddy's attention to it and at once, winter or summer, storm or calm, the dog would plunge in. Once he had saved a child who was in danger of drowning and people had made a fuss and said he ought to have a medal but since no one outside Gaymal got to hear of the rescue and since Gaymal itself forgot the incident within a week or two there never was any medal for the Spuddy to wear on his collar. Apart from the Spuddy's skill at retrieving Joe valued the dog's company because he performed two self-imposed but important tasks on the pier. Firstly he kept all loafing dogs from fouling the boxes of fish that were waiting to be loaded on to the lorries – a job he accomplished with snarling efficiency. Indeed the only time the Spuddy behaved aggressively towards other dogs was when he caught sight of them sniffing too urgently around the full boxes of fish. He ignored their interest in the piles of empty boxes since these would all be hosed clean before being used again but let any dog incautiously loiter too near the full boxes and the Spuddy would be swiftly upon him sending him yelping and racing for safety. His second task was to keep the seagulls away from the newly landed boxes of fish, a task he performed with boisterous venom for if there was anything in this world that the Spuddy had learned to hate it was the omnipresent rapacious gulls. When, among the hurry and bustle of landing fish from the boat, the weighing and auctioning, the gulls converged piratically upon the boxes of silvery fresh fish, the Spuddy would be there leaping with lightning snaps and spitting out feathers while he dodged the beaks that jabbed at him from all sides. He was responsible for many damaged wings among

10

the local gulls and once, when he had caught the wing of a greater black-back and refused to let go, the gull had some-how managed to pull him over the side of the pier and into the harbour. But the Spuddy had held on and, while the fishermen and fishporters ceased work to watch, the contest continued among a great splashing of water and a chorus of cries from the black-back and from spectator gulls. The battle lasted all of five minutes and then the Spuddy, his nose red with his own blood, swam back to the pier steps, leaving the dead black-back floating on the water and the harbour patterned with white gull feathers.

After Joe died the Spuddy appeared to go into semi-retirement, and though he still visited the pier from time to time to assess the activities he usually arrived in the late morning when the boats were at sea and the gulls, either hungry or gorged, arranged themselves in a white frieze along the roof ridges of the sheds and shops that adjoined the pier. It was almost as if he had called a truce with the birds. He still went home for his meal each day as soon as the clock struck twelve just as he had always done with Joe. He continued to sleep on the mat inside the porch, but Marie, who had made no secret of her aversion to dogs, and who had been appalled when Joe had insisted on introducing the Spuddy into the household had, even after four years, conceived no real liking for the dog. For Joe's sake and because she considered it her duty she still put out the Spuddy's meal every day but not for anybody's sake, she vowed, was she going to take him to Glasgow with her.

'You couldn't keep a dog like the Spuddy in a room and kitchen high in a Glasgow tenement,' she told her friends. 'Not even if you wanted to – which she certainly didn't.'

She had made one or two irresolute attempts to give him away but Gaymal was a stony-hearted place where dogs were tolerated as playthings for the children only until the children were of an age to be packed off to school. Then the dogs became a nuisance and were disposed of speedily and without compunction. The few people who professed to like dogs acquired them as status symbols and were unlikely to give a home to a non-thoroughbred. Effie, one of Marie's neighbours, had summed up the problem with soulless clarity.

'What? Give a home to a beast that's as much an accident as a rabbit on the moors?' she had shrilled derisively at Marie's tentative suggestion that she might take the Spuddy. 'Indeed if folks is goin' to be bothered with a dog then they want one that has a decent pedigree so that everyone will know it's cost good money.'

Marie accepted the truth of Effie's assertion. In those days, not long after the war, the fishermen of Gaymal were prosperous and they had to ensure that everything they possessed not only cost money but could be seen to have cost money. 'You'll just have to have him put down before you go,' Effie had insisted. But Marie, briskly matter of fact as she was, somehow recoiled from the idea.

'I don't know indeed,' she said, shaking her head. 'Joe wouldn't have liked me to do that.' The mention of Joe brought tears to her eyes.

'There's nothin' else you can do, is there?' pursued Effie, more gently though at seeing the tears. 'Give him to one of the boats and get them to weight him and throw him overboard when they're well out to sea.'

'It doesn't seem right, that,' objected Marie hesitantly. 'After all, the beast hasn't been much trouble. I think the best thing to do is just to leave him here. He's always been kind of independent and I daresay he'll make out.' She paused, seeing Effie's lips tighten. 'He'd get plenty of offal down at the pier,' she resumed, 'and the boats throw out plenty of food into the harbour he could get for himself. He wouldn't starve.'

12

'If you leave him to stray round here folks will soon get fed up with him an' it won't be long before one of the boats takes him out to make an end of him,' Effie told her. 'You'd best just give him to the Cruelty an' then he'll be off your mind.'

'It seems a shame.' Marie's voice wavered.

Effie glared at her. 'I'm no dog lover myself,' she asserted, 'but to my mind it's not so cruel to have an animal put down as it is to leave him to stray after once givin' him a home.' She turned towards her own front door. 'But I daresay I might just as well save my breath to cool my porridge,' she said as she inserted the key. 'You soft-hearted folks make your own troubles, always takin' the easy way out.' The door closed firmly behind her.

Back in her own kitchen Marie tried to make up her mind whether or not she was going to approach one of the skippers to dispose of the Spuddy. If she just left him and if what Effie had predicted were true then he would end up in the sea anyway. But at least, she told herself, when that happened she wouldn't be there and so have to feel guilty about getting rid of Joe's dog. In the end she decided to leave the Spuddy. She reckoned Effie was right about her being too soft-hearted.

The furniture van had left. The hire car that was to take her on the first stage of her journey had arrived. Marie settled herself in beside the driver, telling him she wished him to get away as quickly as possible and giving an explanatory nod towards the Spuddy who was hovering around as if awaiting the invitation to join her. As the car drew away from the kerb Marie turned to wave to the neighbours who had gathered to see her off. The car reached the end of the street and turned into the main road. The Spuddy stood watching it until it disappeared and sensing the finality of his rejection made no whimper of entreaty or protest. After a few minutes he climbed to the top step of

13

the empty house and lay down, staring along the street, his mixed tobacco brown eyes shadowed with the fatalistic acceptance of his plight. The neighbours lingered gossiping for a while before returning to their own homes. The street became quiet save for the mocking echoes of gull cries carried in by a sea wind. With a sigh the Spuddy's head sank down on to his outstretched paws but his eyes stayed wide and reflective, like those of a man meditating over future plans.

2

When his son was six weeks old skipper Jake's wife announced that she must take the baby home to show him off to her family. 'Home' to Jeannie was the home of her parents, a croft in the outer islands. The home Jake provided for her she always referred to as 'the house'. Jake accepted her announcement impassively. Jeannie was forever making excuses to visit home. Either her father or her mother was ailing and needed her or there was to be a wedding in the family or a relative had just had a baby. In fact Jeannie's relatives made so many demands on her time that in the three years since she had married him Jake doubted if she had spent more than six months with him. It hurt him that she wanted to be away from him so much of the time and he had hoped that when the baby was born she would become more attached, if not to himself, then to the home he worked so hard to give her.

As he came through from the scullery into the kitchen where Jeannie was ironing he was pressing a towel against his newly shaven cheeks and only his eyes betrayed his unhappiness. There were times when Jake thought he ought to put his foot down about Jeannie's frequent absences but he knew in his heart he never would. She was so fair and young and slight and he was so big and swarthy and had such an intimidatingly gruff voice that he was fearful of appearing a bully in her eyes. So he erred on the side of over-indulgence, giving her everything she asked for and never complaining of her lack of interest in him.

'Is the baby old enough to travel?' he asked, trying so hard to keep his voice gentle that it sounded almost meek.

17

'Surely,' returned Jeannie as she guided the iron over the sleeves of a tiny jacket.

'It's just that I've heard folks hereabouts sayin' a baby's not strong enough to take the fresh air until it's six months old,' he persisted, the gruffness edging back into his voice. 'D'you not believe in that yourself?'

Jeannie tossed her head. 'Indeed I believed that when I was younger because that's what the old folks say. Now the nurse says the baby's ready to take fresh air after about two weeks. After all,' she added, 'it isn't as if it's the winter time yet.'

Jake went over to the cot in the corner of the kitchen and lifting the coverlet gazed down at his sleeping son. His sad, tight mouth relaxed into a tender smile. Was he going to see as little of his son as he did of his wife, he wondered bitterly and looked across at Jeannie who with her back to him was still ironing. She had once seemed so shy and desirable with her clear smooth skin and glossy hair but soon after they married he noticed her shyness had given way to an almost vixen-like quality and though her complexion and hair remained as attractive as ever he rarely saw her other than as she was now in carpet slippers and overall with her hair confined in a structure of steel curlers. He let himself wish that she would dress herself up for him when he came home at weekends. But she never did. When he went away to sea on Monday mornings her hair was in curlers and when he came home on Friday nights it was still in curlers. For only about two hours on a Sunday was her hair unconfined and then, because she was going to church, it was hidden under her hat. However, this was not all that disturbed him, for it seemed that she found an awful lot of housework to do at weekends when he was at home and while he admitted it was nice to know he had a clean shining home he would have preferred it to be a place where he could relax and rest his body from the constant swing of the sea: a place where he would be greeted by a neatly dressed wife prepared to share with him the comfort of their own fireside with perhaps later a few of the neighbours dropping in for a wee dram and a 'wee crack' and a discussion of the week's fishing. Like most fishermen he had a strong streak of romanticism and when he was first married he had dreamed of the weekend respites from the discomfort of the boat: of returning and opening the door of his welcoming home to call 'I'm back, Jeannie!'; of finding her in his arms; of lifting her up and carrying her to the kitchen. But even before he had touched her she had seen the eagerness in his eyes and had evaded him. 'She didn't like that sort of thing,' she had rebuffed him. 'It was soft.' Now at weekends he returned either to a listless greeting and the bustle of housework; the moving of furniture that she was unable to move by herself; the careful treading over newspapers that covered the constantly washed floors, or else too frequently he returned to a house that was clean and shining but was cold and empty and there would be a note on the table saying: 'Have gone home – mother not keeping well'. At first she had stayed away only two or three weeks at a time but then her absences grew to months and he realised that except for financial support there was little else she wanted from him. He wondered if she wanted what any man could give her since island girls had a reputation for making their first duty the wellbeing of their parents. No matter what other commitments a woman might have she had from childhood been so indoctrinated with the belief that her loyalty was to her parents and to the homestead where she herself had been born and reared that she cleaved more naturally to them than to her husband.

Gently Jake replaced the coverlet over his son. He cleared his throat. 'I'd like to see a fair bit of the boy, Jeannie' he said.

'And when would you see him anyway?' Jeannie taunted. 'With you away at the fishing all week it's precious little you see of your own house let alone your son.'

'But Jeannie!' he expostulated. 'I've to earn money for us, haven't I? An' how else would I do it except for the fishin'?' He knew just how much money he had to earn to keep up with Jeannie's whims. She tired of things so quickly, forever demanding change and he reckoned they had bought enough to furnish three homes in the time they had been married. Only he knew how he hated to have to call out his crew in weather that made other skippers comment: 'It's only greed or need that would make a man go out to sea on a day like this.'

Jeannie shrugged. 'Well, what sort of a life d'you think it is for me here all by myself with a man only coming home at weekends and him only wanting his bed then.'

'But the other wives are the same,' he pointed out. 'A fisherman's wife knows what to expect before she marries him.'

'Well, I can't help it if I like company,' she retorted. 'It's what I'm used to.'

'Can you not make friends with the other women?' he asked. 'They'd be company for you.'

'Ach, they're that proud,' she said defensively. 'They're not my own folk.'

'Aye, right enough they're not,' said Jake resignedly. 'But all the same I'm sayin' I'd like to see my son growin' up and there'll not be much chance for me to do that if you have him away at your parents as much as you have been yourself. I'm askin' you not to stay away so long.'

'That'll depend on how my father's keeping.' Jeannie's voice sparked at him like sticks on a newly lit fire. 'He wasn't keeping so well in my mother's last letter,' she added. She thumped the iron down and started to gather up the pile of clothes.

Jake looked at her, dismayed as always by her apparent renunciation of him but he was too proud and thought of himself as being too inarticulate to plead with her further. He opened a cupboard and took out some tools.

'Which is the shelf you say you want fixin'?'' he asked her in a tired voice.

3

While Marie Glenn was speeding away from Gaymal another car was speeding towards the village. In this car there were again only two occupants, the driver himself and sitting beside him a boy of about eight years old who stared out at the passing landscape with wide inscrutable eyes. The boy's name was Andy but he could not have told anyone that for though he was a good looking boy, well grown and sturdy with curly fair hair and large eyes the colour of fresh cut peat, he was completely dumb. When people first saw Andy they tended to exclaim admiringly: 'That's a grand looking boy!' but when they realised he could not speak they would add: 'Ach, the poor thing's a dummy!' And Andy, whose hearing was at least as good as theirs, winced at their pity as if it had been abuse. From the time he had been able to understand the speech of adults and had thus become aware of his own affliction he had begun to feel excluded even from his own parents. His father was in the merchant navy and was away for long periods leaving Andy and his mother on their own. But their being together had not resulted in togetherness for once Andy had outgrown the toddler stage, ceasing for her to be an absorbing interest, she had become withdrawn. Not that she displayed any lack of affection towards the boy. On the contrary she was at times demonstrative. She had even spared the time to teach him to write his name and had encouraged his love of drawing, buying vast quantities of paper and crayons to keep him occupied. But when she was not being demonstrative she appeared indifferent, even a little resentful towards him and as he grew older Andy sensed that his muteness embarrassed her. He thought he understood. She was a vivacious woman liking the company of the many friends who called while leaving Andy to sit quietly in a corner of the room drawing the boats he loved. As he listened to the lively chatter and banter and thought how much prettier his mother was than all the other women he wondered if like him she was wishing, deep down, that his father's leave would soon be due and they could all three be together. But there came a time when, Andy noticed, the number of friends being entertained dwindled until there were only two or three and finally one, a man, and when he came his mother insisted on Andy going to bed.

When the telegram arrived announcing his father's imminent arrival, instead of grabbing Andy's arms and exuberantly dancing him around the room his mother rushed upstairs and began packing suitcases. Coming down again she said in reply to Andy's look of bewilderment: 'I'm going away for a bit.' Her voice was strained. She gave him no further explanation but told him not to go out until his father arrived, and added that there was a cold lunch prepared for them both in the larder. Then she put an envelope beside the clock on the mantelpiece. 'See your father reads that when he comes,' she told him. She was frowning in an abstracted way and her eyes were bright. As she moved past him Andy put a hand on her arm and looked at her imploringly. 'I can't stay, Andy,' she said in a tight voice. 'It's no good. I just can't stay.' His hand slid down to his side. 'Be a good boy,' she said, giving him a quick hug. The door closed behind her and she was running down the garden path and out to the car where a man was waiting. She did not glance back or wave at her son who stood forlornly holding aside the curtain watching his mother go.

Even when his father arrived and enveloped him in a huge hug Andy did not break down but only pointed to the letter on the mantelpiece. With a half quizzical glance at Andy as if he suspected a joke his father took the letter and sat down to read it. After he had read and re-read it he stood up and put a hand on Andy's shoulder. 'Your mother's gone away for a wee whiley,' he said thickly. 'I expect she told you. It's your granny, she's not keepin' so well. I daresay she'll be back soon.' He didn't look at Andy as he spoke. 'Now I'm just going upstairs for a wee kip and when I come down again we'll put on our best bibs and tuckers and go out somewhere, eh?' He was too distressed to see his son's anxious eyes following him out of the kitchen.

Andy stood desolate. He had wanted his father to talk to him: to admit that his mother had left them for someone she liked better and not try to fob him off with a lie about Granny. He knew what had happened and he wanted his father to share their mutual knowledge and their grief; he felt they ought to have been able to comfort each other. His shoulders sagged. It seemed that even in this moment of crisis his dumbness was still a barrier; that even his own father accepted that an inability to speak meant a similar inability to understand and even feel or share emotion. Andy got out his paper and crayons but he found he did not want to draw. He wandered into the larder and looked at the food but he had no desire to eat. He had no desire for anything – not even to go out as his father had promised, because of a fear that if they left the house it and all the other familiar things would not be there when they returned. Not knowing what to do with himself he went at last and sat on the bottom stair, hugging his knees and listening for a sign of movement from his father.

When his father did come down, determinedly bright and talkative, they went out despite Andy's reluctance to leave the house and for the ensuing six weeks of his father's leave they did more things together than they had ever done before. There were trips by rail and by bus; walking in the country; fishing; taking meals in restaurants, so filling Andy's days with new experiences that at night he was too tired to brood for long.

The day came when his father began preparations to return to his ship.

'Tomorrow,' he said in reply to Andy's questioning glance. He knelt down and putting an arm round the boy he went on. 'I've fixed up for you to go and stay for a little while with your Aunt Sarah and Uncle Ben. You've never seen her but she's seen photographs of you and she's taken a real fancy to you.' His father's arm tightened around him. 'And there's Uncle Ben. You'll like him. He doesn't draw boats like you but he builds them. They live at Gaymal where there are plenty of boats. You'll be able to go down to the pier whenever you like and draw as many as you've a mind.' He looked into Andy's eyes. 'You'll like that, won't you?'

Andy nodded and managed a faint smile.

'Aye, and you'll be able to get on board one or two of the fishing boats for a trip if you've got good sea legs, which you ought to have, boy, seeing you're the son of a sailor.' Andy knew his father was wanting him to show enthusiasm so he responded as best he could. He dreaded the idea of leaving home and going to live with strange people even if they were relatives but he knew there was no alternative.

'There's a car coming for us both tomorrow and I'll ride with you part of the way,' his father continued. 'I wanted to come with you all the way and see you settled in but my leave's been chopped a bit. The idea now is that this car will take us to the docks where my ship is and you'll be able to see me go aboard before you set off for Aunt Sarah's.' Andy nodded and again forced a faint smile. 'So off you go up to your bedroom and pack up anything you want to take. Mrs Peake next door is coming in to pack

28

your clothes and things but you'll be wanting to take your paper and crayons and a good few of your sketches, eh?'

As Andy went slowly up the stairs to his bedroom his father stood staring after him, asking himself whether it would be more heartrending to have a son who could confide in words his fear and dejection rather than one like Andy who could only convey it by the slump of his body and the anguish in his eyes.

Andy had seen his father's ship; watched his father stride up the gangplank and turn and wave before disappearing from sight. Then the driver had said very firmly that they must continue their journey if they were to reach Gaymal before dark. The driver was very kind to Andy, inviting him to sit at the front with him and pointing out so many interesting things that the boy had little time to be miserable. Shortly after five o'clock the car entered Gaymal and pulled up in front of a house three doors away from Marie Glenn's former home.

4

The Spuddy still lay on the top step of the empty house having returned there after seeking out the dinner Marie had conscientiously left for him in his bowl beside the coal shed. Marie had always put his dinner beside the coal shed and the Spuddy would watch her doing it although he always waited until the church clock struck twelve before he would approach and start to eat. Always that is unless the church clock happened to be slow for it seemed his own time was more accurate than mechanical time. If Joe ever spotted the Spuddy eating his dinner before the clock struck he would switch on the wireless to check the time so that he could report to Danny, whose responsibility it was to regulate the clock.

The Spuddy watched the car arrive as he had watched every other activity in the street since Marie had left. He saw the boy alight and be greeted warmly by his aunt; he saw them go into the house for a while and then come out again, when the driver got into the car and drove away, leaving the boy and his aunt standing on the pavement. The woman moved towards the house calling to Andy but he had noticed the empty looking house and the Spuddy lying there alone and ran after her, pulling at her sleeve while gesticulating towards the dog. The Spuddy affected not to notice their interest as the woman, pausing to explain, shook her head disapprovingly in the Spuddy's direction. She disappeared inside, gesturing the boy to follow, but Andy did not go immediately. With his hands grasping the pointed railings that divided his aunt's garden from her neighbour's he leaned over and stared fixedly at the dog until the Spuddy's head came round and he returned the boy's stare with a long glance of interest.

At tea time when Aunt Sarah wasn't looking Andy managed to slip a couple of slices of bread and a sausage into his pocket. Since his aunt had explained that the Spuddy had been abandoned he had resolved that he himself must try to feed the dog. He estimated that if his aunt regularly put as much food on the table as she had this evening he wouldn't have much difficulty in providing for the Spuddy. After tea while his aunt was in the kitchen washing the dishes he slipped out into the dusk and sped quietly to the gate of the empty house. Not knowing for certain whether or not the dog was savage Andy held out a hunk of bread before daring to open the gate and when the Spuddy ignored the offering he pulled the greasy cold sausage from his pocket and waved it about, hoping the dog would smell the appetising meatiness and be tempted to come for it. The Spuddy, having eaten his one accustomed meal of the day, was not hungry and refused to show any interest. All the same he was intrigued. The Spuddy had never regarded himself as being a child's dog. Children were noisy and excitable and he preferred to evade their approaches but though he could recall young boys trying to cajole him with soft words or to command him with curses the patient mute overtures of this boy baffled him and he continued regarding him with aloof enquiry, making no movement as he saw him unlatch the gate, sidle through and advance tentatively up the path towards him. Andy held out the sausage but the Spuddy still disdained it and the boy's friendly expression changed to one of disappointment. Andy put down a piece of bread and the sausage on the ground beside the Spuddy but still they were ignored. Venturing closer he held out a hand, palm outstretched, hoping the dog would sniff it and realising it was the hand of a friend would perhaps even give a lick of acceptance. The Spuddy looked at the hand and looked

34

away again. He was not in the habit of licking hands let alone strange ones: it would have been too much like an act of submission. To Andy the Spuddy seemed to be spurning his offer of friendship. He slumped down on the bottom step looking up at the dog in the gathering dark waiting for some reciprocal gesture of comradeship and when it did not come his head drooped forward until it was resting on his arms and his shoulders began to shake with the sobs that had for so long been wanting to escape from his body. Only then did the Spuddy weaken. Moving down to the bottom step he sat down and laid a paw gently on the boy's neck, glancing about him as he did so as if he was afraid someone might witness his unwonted display of tenderness. He need not have worried. By now it was quite dark and there was no sound in the street until a door opened and Andy heard his aunt calling him.

5

All that night the Spuddy lay on the steps of his former home but when the first fingers of light reached over the shoulders of the hills he got up, stretched himself and sauntered away down the street. Andy, coming out of his aunt's house after breakfast, was disappointed at not seeing the dog and resolved to go and look for him. Since he did not know his own way about Gaymal Andy had no idea where he should look but nevertheless he set out with that intention and as all Gaymal roads led inevitably towards the harbour it was on the pier that he eventually found himself. He stared in wonder. He had visited docks with his father but busy and exciting as they had seemed to him he now thought of them as being landlocked and lethargic in comparison with the spectacle of Gaymal. There was so much sea everywhere, so much sky and colour and movement and he could only stand letting the sights and sounds and the smells of the harbour envelop and enthrall him. He forgot his intention of looking for the Spuddy; forgot the ache of depression that had been with him during the past few weeks. He even forgot for the time that he was dumb since everyone was so busy and there was so much noise that people tended to gesticulate rather than talk. Here were boats galore: herring boats landing their catches; launches loading supplies; the lifeboat swinging at its moorings, and at the end of the pier the steamer was hauling up its gangplanks preparatory to leaving. The raucous siren announcing its intention of doing so seemed to Andy to be lifting the upper half of his body from the lower half and he pressed his hands over his ears to deaden the noise. Passing fishporters observing him threw him friendly grins and Andy grinned back ecstatically. He picked his way among all the fish boxes, trolleys, barrels, hoses and ropes that go to make up the impedimenta of a fish pier, his shoes scrunching on pieces of crab shell or skidding on fish that had been pulped to slime by the wheels of the lorries, until he reached the end of the pier. The steamer was well away now leaving a wake like a discarded shawl as it sailed into a misty rainbow that arched itself across the distant islands. Andy watched until steamer wake and rainbow vanished behind a gauzy screen of rain when, suddenly realising that the rain was now sweeping in over the pier and that he himself was getting wet, he ran for the meagre shelter of a high-piled stack of fish boxes where he waited until the shower had passed before continuing along a path between more stacks of fish boxes which brought him into the boatyard where his Uncle Ben worked. As his father had predicted Andy had taken an immediate liking to Uncle Ben. He quite liked his aunt but whereas Aunt Sarah was all scuttle and sharp-tongued splutter Uncle Ben was slow with smiling eyes and more given to expressing himself by nodding his head than by speaking. When he was not eating Uncle Ben had his pipe in his mouth and the only time he had conversed with Andy so far was when he had taken out the pipe to refill or relight it. He had said little then but his voice was gentle and the words comforting. Andy felt his uncle understood and he began to feel safe again. He thought that some day he might even show Uncle Ben some of his drawings – an honour so far reserved for his parents.

Andy found his uncle working on a fishing boat that was winched high on the slip: a boat that had hit a rock, his uncle explained, and had needed several planks renewing. She's been lucky, his uncle told him, if the weather had worsened the boat could easily have become a total wreck before the lifeboat reached her and the crew could have lost their lives. As he was speaking his uncle's hands were caressing the boat's side with as much tenderness as a mother smoothing a cot sheet over a sleeping child. Andy, who had never before seen anything bigger than a dinghy completely out of the water was overwhelmed by the sheer size of the underside of the boat. Standing beneath her and letting his eyes run along the generous curve of the bilge; the sweep of the hull into the keel; the sweet run of the seams, and the whole resulting in an impression of rightness; of strength and of fitness for the continual combat with the sea, he thought how beautiful she was. Uncle Ben, who had been observing him, took his pipe out of his mouth to say, 'Aye, a boat's a beautiful thing, boy,' to which Andy replied by running his own hands along the planks and smiling rapt agreement. He knew now that no longer would he be content to draw boats: he wanted to go to sea and he wanted to go in a boat just like this one he was admiring.

The church clock striking twelve reminded them it was time for their dinner and in the leisurely way of a devoted craftsman Uncle Ben put away his tools. Together they left the slip, climbed up to the quay and made for home. As they turned into the street the first thing Andy saw was a large van parked outside the empty house and men unloading furniture from it. 'Where's the Spuddy?' he thought in a panic and was angry with himself for having forgotten his intention of looking for the dog. Andy dawdled, letting his uncle go in front of him. He stood by the gate gaping at the activity. Foolishly he had let himself think that the house would remain empty; that the Spuddy would continue to visit and sleep there and thus be accessible to further overtures of friendship. But new people meant complications. New people might have a dog of their own or they might dislike dogs altogether and what would happen then? It was at that moment he saw the Spuddy.

The Spuddy had spent the morning doing his usual rounds of the pier and the kipper yard but when he had heard the clock strike twelve habit had turned him in the direction of his former home. He was not expecting to find his meal put out for him but he thought he might just as well make sure. When he saw the furniture van and strange people going in and out of the house he had sufficient intelligence to realise he was unlikely to be welcome there but he felt he could risk slipping round to the back to see if his bowl was in the accustomed place beside the coal shed. It was, but it was empty of everything save a few drops of rain and the lingering smell of yesterday's food. He licked it more to assert ownership than for the meat-tainted moisture but even as he did so a red-haired woman appeared and amid a shrill stream of invective hurled a stone which hit the path beside him. Ruffled but still dignified the Spuddy retreated to the other side of the street and at what he judged to be a safe distance he sat down to keep an eye on the proceedings. As he did so there was a clang against the kerb a few feet away from him. It was his empty feeding bowl. The Spuddy was still sitting there, half obscured by the bulky van, when Andy spotted him. Immediately he ran towards him and putting a gentle hand on the dog's head crouched down and let his arm slide down until it was around the dog's neck. The Spuddy's response was a cursory lick on the ear which might have become more fervent had not the red-haired woman emerged from the house to scream at Andy not to encourage the beast. She wasn't going to have it hanging around her place, she yelled, as she re-entered the house and shut the door. Andy, catching sight of the empty bowl in the gutter and guessing why it was there knew that unless he could help him the Spuddy was going to be in a hazardous position. As he retrieved the bowl he heard his aunt's voice scolding him for his slowness and urging him to

42

come for his dinner. With an encouraging pat on the Spuddy's head Andy left him and followed his aunt inside. When the meal was over and she had cleared away he showed her the Spuddy's empty bowl, mutely asking her for scraps.

'Indeed no!' she declared firmly. 'I'm not giving you food to take to that dog. He should have been put down before his own folks went away and it's only a matter of time before he's put down anyway.' She put her hands on her hips and looked hard at Andy. 'If you go tempting him to hang round here you'll upset the neighbours and I won't stand for that. Anyway,' she went on, 'the more you tempt him the more likely it's you yourself will be the death of him. Aye, you, Andy,' she stressed, seeing his look of consternation. 'The woman that's moving in to the house was here taking a cup of tea with me earlier this morning and she canna abide dogs at any price, she was telling me. She's that nervous of them, she says, and if the Spuddy still comes round now that she's moved in her husband's going to complain to the police.' She gathered up the tablecloth. 'Aye, and then something will have to be done about getting rid of him.' She went to the back door, shook the crumbs from the cloth and coming back in said less severely: 'The best thing you can do for that dog, Andy, is to keep away from him and make sure he keeps away from you.' Out of the corner of his eye Andy saw Uncle Ben nodding sad confirmation.

Dejectedly tucking the bowl under his anorak Andy went out into the street but the moment he saw the Spuddy again his dejection became resolution. The Spuddy and he were going to be friends and somehow friends must contrive to look after each other. It wouldn't be easy – that much he knew – but if only he could keep the Spuddy fed and unharmed until his father came on leave he was certain his father would find some way of ensuring that Andy could keep the dog. Sadness descended on him as he wished, as so often before, that he could correspond with his father; that he could read and write like other children of his age and thus be able to both send and receive letters. But when his father was at sea their communication with each other was limited to picture postcards with lots of X's printed clearly on the back which his father posted whenever he was in port. In reply Andy could only add more X's together with a painstakingly printed 'ANDY' to his mother's letters and sometimes give her one of his drawings to enclose.

Shaking off his despondency Andy approached the Spuddy and showing him the feeding bowl tried to entice the dog to follow him but the Spuddy, used to verbal invitations and instructions, was reluctant until Andy's explicit gestures, aided by a renewal of invective from the red-haired woman persuaded him to accompany the boy. Before leaving the house Andy had checked the money in his pocket and money being something his mother had ensured he was familiar with he reckoned he had enough to be able to buy at least two and perhaps three days food for the Spuddy, and today being a Wednesday it was only three days before he was due for another week's pocket money from the sum his father had left for that purpose.

Pausing outside the butcher's he looked in at the window but he thought the butcher looked harassed and loath to risk adding to his harassment by trying to convey by signs what he wished to purchase he chose instead to go to the general store where it was relatively easy for him to point to a tin of dog meat and a tin opener, hand over the requisite money and skip away. If he was aware of the mystified shopkeeper coming to the doorway to observe him further Andy gave no sign and together he and the Spuddy raced towards a promising looking huddle of sheds which he had noticed earlier in the morning. Here Andy felt sure he would be able to find a quiet corner where he could stand guard whilst the Spuddy ate his meal. The sheds, he discovered, were situated within the kipper yard itself, a place where it was obvious the Spuddy was completely at home. It was in fact the Spuddy who led Andy to where two small and patently disused sheds abutted to form a reasonably secluded spot and, watched closely by the Spuddy, Andy set the feeding bowl on the ground, opened the tin and tipped the contents into the bowl, pushing it towards the dog and nodding vigorously as he did so. The Spuddy regarded the boy in the same dubious manner as a shopkeeper might regard an urchin who has offered him a five pound note to change. His glance dropped to the food and his nose twitched. With diminished uncertainty yet still without complete conviction his glance returned to the boy. Andy pushed the bowl nearer; he lifted it up and held it close to the dog's nose before putting it down again and only then did the Spuddy, with a dignified swing of his tail which Andy interpreted as a gracious 'thank you', begin to eat. Crouching with his back against the wall of the shed Andy smiled with satisfaction.

The next thing he must do for the Spuddy, Andy resolved, was to try to find a place where the dog might sleep unmolested at nights. While Andy was disposing of the empty meat tin by tossing it into the harbour and while he washed the feeding bowl under the tap on the pier he pondered over his problem. One of the empty sheds where he had fed the dog was a possibility but where and how he would get sacks or some other form of bedding to cover the damp-looking earth floor? When you were unable to speak it was difficult to indicate even the simplest things you wanted. How was he to mime to strangers his request for bedding for a dog he was not supposed to have? All afternoon the boy and the dog roamed Gaymal but when tea-time came Andy had still found neither bedding nor a cosier alternative to the shed for his companion.

The evening dusk was thickening and since his aunt had stipulated that he must be home by dark he knew the time had come when he must leave the Spuddy. Clapping his hands he gestured towards the kipper yard but the Spuddy stayed beside him. He tried stamping his feet; a pretence of kicking and of throwing. He tried dodging and hiding but the Spuddy was not to be diverted. Feeling traitorous Andy at last picked up a stone and throwing it so as not to hit the dog he made what he hoped was a menacing rush towards him. The Spuddy was surprised but not deterred. Andy grew desperate but it was Uncle Ben coming home from work who solved the problem for him. 'Way back, boy!' he commanded the Spuddy. 'Way back! You mustn't come near this place. Go!' His voice was quietly authoritative and the dog, understanding at last, turned away and loped off in the direction of the kipper yard. Miserably Andy wondered if the Spuddy would ever come near him again but the next morning when he rounded the corner into the main road there was the Spuddy waiting for him as gladly as if he recalled nothing of their parting. Always after that when Andy had to return to his aunt's house the Spuddy escorted him until they had almost reached the street when he would stop and allow Andy to go on without him. When Andy came out again the Spuddy would be waiting to greet him and where he spent the intervening time Andy never discovered.

6

It seemed to Andy that the days raced by with the speed of the wind-chased wavelets he liked to watch rolling past the end of the pier and so captivated was he by the kaleidoscopic pageantry of the harbour he had little time to dwell on the crisis which had brought him to Gaymal. For the first few weeks after his arrival he had looked every morning to see if the postman had brought him word from his mother – perhaps a picture postcard like those his father sent him with lots of X's on the back to let him know she still loved him but as the days became weeks and there was still no sign from her he began to accept that either she had forgotten him or she wished him to forget her. If he could not make himself forget her he did at least succeed in decolourizing his memories of her sufficiently to open his eyes to the affection that was being offered to him in his new surroundings. The Spuddy's attachment to him was unmistakable and Uncle Ben made no secret of the warmth of his feelings and even his aunt, whose testiness had once unnerved him, began to betray a hitherto unsuspectedly tender side to her nature. Sarah had never had any wish to appear forbidding but she was a congenitally fussy woman and having no children of her own she had not relished the prospect of taking Andy into her home. She had done it, she confided to her husband and to her neighbours, because she considered it her duty and though this was undoubtedly true Andy had not been in her care for more than a few weeks before she was admitting to herself that she hoped his father's voyage would be a prolonged one.

She began to consider the boy's education, complaining

to Ben that it had been wickedly neglected; she rowed with the local schoolmaster when he refused, because of Andy's affliction, to take him into the school as a pupil and when the darker evenings brought long hours indoors she determined that she herself would be Andy's tutor. Confiding this intention to a friend who also happened to be the school cleaner she induced him to 'borrow' some lesson books so that she could teach Andy to read and write. Despite a scolding tongue she displayed not only a natural ability to teach but also an astonishing patience with the boy and, stimulated by his keenness to learn, she tended to ignore most of the chores she normally felt compelled to undertake in the evenings so as to devote the time to Andy and his studies, with the result that at the end of three months Andy found he could write to his father giving him the glorious news that if his father wrote a letter in return he would now be able to read it for himself.

During all the hours of daylight Andy and the Spuddy were down at the pier, mingling with the fish porters and watching the comings and goings of the boats. His eye was becoming trained to the lines of boats and to their different responses to the sea so that he could recognize each boat long before it reached the harbour. He knew most of the crews and was accustomed to being thrown a rope to hitch round a bollard or being told to bring a hose or even being called aboard to collect the empty pop bottles to take to the grocer with the instruction that he could keep the 'penny backs' for himself. Andy was glad of the 'penny backs' because they helped him to buy more food for the Spuddy and so augment the scraps he saved from his own meals. Uncle Ben helped too by saving his own scraps and if Aunt Sarah ever noticed the total lack of food on her table at the end of their meals she made no comment. So long as Andy did not offend the neighbours by allowing the Spuddy to hang round the place she felt it right to hold her tongue. After all, she conceded, maybe a dumb boy needed a dumb friend and at least the dog kept Andy out all day so that he wasn't constantly under her feet.

After a long lingering autumn winter howled in with wild sharp-toothed winds that scraped the skin like a steel comb. The hills which had been snow-capped became snow shawled and soon snow-skirted; the pier puddles were skimmed with ice and fishermen and porters flapped their arms across their oilskinned bodies trying to keep warm during the minutes of inaction. Andy, snug in the thick sweaters his aunt knitted for him and in the 'oilies' she had bought for him began to worry anew over the Spuddy's sleeping quarters. He suspected that wherever the Spuddy spent his nights it was too exposed a place for him to withstand the severity of winter. There were mornings when the dog's coat was unaccountably wet and one day Andy noticed him shivering a lot. The next morning, after a night of blizzard, Andy found the Spuddy waiting for him in snow that was up to his belly; his ears were drooping and snow from the last flurry was still melting in his coat. Andy was sure the Spuddy was sick and resolved to go to Uncle Ben and somehow persuade him to help find a safe, warm place for the Spuddy to sleep. Down at the boatyard Uncle Ben watched Andy's passionately expressive mime with complete understanding and after feeling the dog's hot nose and cold ears he led them to the far corner of the work-shed where there was a great pile of wood shavings and cotton waste. Andy looked at his uncle with grateful comprehension and began to arrange the shavings into a nest-like hollow which he lined with cotton waste. Even before he had finished the Spuddy, without waiting to be invited, stepped into the centre of the nest, turned round twice and settled himself down with an audible sigh of relief. For three days the Spuddy hardly stirred from his new bed but lay there showing little interest in anything, even food, and Andy, fearing his friend might die, stayed miserably around the boat shed, rarely leaving it except at his uncle's insistence. On the fourth day when the Spuddy saw Andy he got up out of his bed to greet him. On the fifth day he was prepared to accompany Andy down to the pier and on the sixth day Andy was overjoyed to find the Spuddy waiting for him in the usual place near the main road. But henceforth instead of the Spuddy escorting Andy most of the way home in the evenings it was Andy who escorted the Spuddy to the boatyard and saw him comfortably settled in his quarters.

7

For skipper Jake and the crew of the 'Silver Crest' the fishing season had proved a disastrous one. It had begun with a broken con rod in the engine which kept them tied up at the pier for close on two weeks and when that was repaired there had followed a run of bad luck which included fouled nets, a seized winch and gear damaged by heavy seas. When at last they managed to get a good spell at sea they found the herring shoals elusive and instead of 'Silver Crest' coming into port with fish holds so full that skipper and crew felt justified in taking a few hours rest and relaxation she was arriving with a meagre cran or two which necessitated their turning round straight away after unloading and going back to sea to search for new grounds to set their nets, perhaps snatching only two hours rest out of the twenty-four. From being one of the highest earning boats in the port they had dropped to being one of the lowest – a source of chagrin for any skipper with pride. The crew were dispirited and worried by the superstition that the bad luck which was dogging them might yet bring worse catastrophe. But Jake dismissed their fears. Despite discomforts, disappointments and danger he would allow nothing to affect his driving ambition to catch fish – more and more fish to earn more and more money for himself and his crew. And since Jeannie, his wife, was so much away from home visiting her parents Jake was also goaded by loneliness – loneliness and the recurring pain in his stomach which only hard work or deep sleep could dull.

Before he had met Jeannie, Jake, in common with most Gaymal fishermen, had been a heavy drinker, spending all his weekends ashore in the local pub downing whisky after whisky and when the pain had first insinuated itself into his stomach he had drunk even more whisky in the hope of alleviating it. Eventually its acuteness had driven him to see his doctor.

'You'll have to keep off the drink,' the doctor warned after examining him. 'I can give you medicine but medicine can't fight the damage the whisky's doing you. It would be different if you took a bit more care of yourself but ach!' The doctor shook his head. 'You fishermen are all the same. You abuse your bodies all week, working like galley slaves, going without sleep and bolting great wads of stodgy food and when the weekend comes you're away to the pub and pouring whisky into your stomach as if it was an empty barrel with holes in the bottom.'

Jake had intended to heed the doctor's warning but Gaymal offered only two places where an unmarried man ashore for the weekend could find company and relaxation. They were the pub and a district up at the back of the kipper yards locally known as 'Chinatown' where the itinerant 'kipper lassies' had their quarters. Jake had nothing against the kipper lassies; indeed he preferred them to the local girls who, he considered, suffered too much from what he called the 'I want disease', but not being by nature a wenching man he had settled for the pub and since neither the Gaymal pub nor its customers welcomed teetotallers nor even moderate imbibers Jake had continued his drinking. Continued that is until Jeannie had come into his life.

From the day he had first seen her behind the counter in the local paper shop he had wanted her for his wife. Her smallness and primness delighted him and he liked to observe her pretending to frown at the teasing remarks of the fishermen while all the time, the enamoured Jake was sure, she was really finding it difficult to restrain her demure little mouth from breaking into a smile. He reckoned she was about half his age and he wondered if she would think him too old for her so he was both astounded and delighted when she responded to his first tentative approaches and when, after they had known each other for about two months, she agreed to accompany him on a visit to his sister in Glasgow he felt the time had come for him to ask her to marry him. As they wandered with apparent aimlessness along the city streets Jake intentionally edged her towards the windows of jewellers' shops and when she had exclaimed over the displays of rings he suggested with stumbling diffidence that he should buy her one as an engagement ring. She had declined at first as he had expected her to but noting the sparkle in her eyes when she studied the rings he could see the temptation was strong and when he pressed a little she soon yielded. He was earning good money at that time and the ring they chose was an expensive one; so also were the coat and jersey and skirt which she fell in love with and which he, in a glow of devotion, insisted she should have. What did it matter if he spent in a single night what had taken him a month to earn? He had a boat, hadn't he? And there were plenty more shoals of herring in the sea waiting to be caught.

The change Jeannie had brought into his life had been at first dramatic. In her company he found it easy to stifle the urge to drink and during their courtship and the early weeks of their marriage and even during her first two or three absences from home Jake steadfastly renounced his visits to the pub with the result that not only was his pain less constant but his whole body reacted with a renewed vitality that reminded him of his youth. When Jeannie's visits to her parents became more frequent and more prolonged Jake, disillusioned as to her feelings for him and hating the emptiness of the house at weekends, relapsed into his former ways, beginning by drinking himself into a confusion of thought that he hoped he might mistake for happiness and culminating at closing time when he staggered home from the pub to drop on his bed in a stupor of intoxication through which the pain bored itself inexorably. In an effort to deaden the pain he conjured up the image of his wife's pale face, framed as he liked best to recall it by long tresses of her fine hair and, as drowsiness teased him he saw that her face was floating on the sea and her hair had woven itself into a net – strong net – fishing net in which several replicas of her face were caught and, as the net was hauled in through the swirling water to break surface there were hundreds more replicas and the hundreds became thousands and were no longer faces but herring – the 'silver darlings': huge bursting netfulls of them pouring in a writhing, leaping, coruscating stream over the side of the boat and into the hold. Jake tried to clear his befuddled brain. If ever a fisherman needs to woo sleep he does not do so by counting sheep going through a gate but by counting herring: baskets and baskets of herring, cascading into the hold. How many? Again and again Jake tried to estimate but perversely, as always, sleep overtook him before he could calculate the worth of the catch in hard cash.

8

It was in the early hours of a Monday morning after just such a heavy weekend that Jake, grey-faced and bloodshot eyed, came down to the boat. The crew glanced at him with concern before turning to grimace at one another but they waited until they were gathered in the fo'c'sle and Jake was still in the wheelhouse before they commented on his appearance.

'A drink's a drink,' burst out the youngest member of the crew indignantly. 'But the skipper's killin' himself with it.'

'It's that wife of his who's killin' him if anybody is,' supplied another. 'She knows fine he goes on the batter whenever she's away from him. But she won't stay, not her.'

'He's too good to her, that's what's wrong,' put in the cook.

'It's just not decent the way she leaves him,' said the youngest member again. 'If she was mine I'd take my belt to her.'

'Island women!' exclaimed another. 'That's them all over.' The speaker was an east coast man and found the islanders utterly baffling.

'It's a bloody shame!' the young man continued. 'He's a damn good skipper an' I don't like to see him made so little of by a woman.' He frowned. 'Particularly now he has the bairn,' he added.

It was the oldest member of the crew who corrected him. 'It's herself has the bairn,' he said quietly. 'An' I'm thinkin' there's little Jake will get to see of him now she's got away with him.'

As he spoke there was an ominous clanking noise. The

engine slowed, then ceased altogether. They rushed up on deck to see the skipper coming out of the wheelhouse.

'Take the boat!' he shouted at the man nearest to him. 'That blasted engine's done the dirty on us again.' He ran quickly down to the engine room. The old man looked at the cook. 'That's it, then,' he observed. 'It seems as if our bad luck's not done with us yet.'

After an hour or so of wrestling with the engine Jake managed to coax enough power for them to labour back into port where a worried looking engineer was waiting for them on the pier. Together he and Jake inspected the engine while the crew waited gloomily wondering how long they were going to be delayed. The engineer came up on deck followed by a glowering Jake. 'Not before midnight,' he was saying as he wiped his hands on a bunch of cotton waste. 'Not a hope.' As one man the crew set off in the direction of the pub.

For Andy also the day had begun bleakly. Uncle Ben after much apologetic head shaking had warned him that his boss was insisting that the workshed where the Spuddy slept must be cleaned out and all the shavings and waste disposed of by the end of the week. There was to be no bed for the Spuddy at the boatyard any more and neither he nor his uncle could think of an alternative. Pottering miserably around the pier wrestling with the problem he was there to witness the unexpected return of the 'Silver Crest' and anxious to know the cause of it he ran down to watch her tying up.

Of all the boats coming in and going out of the harbour Andy thought the 'Silver Crest' the most beautiful in shape and the best cared for. Empty or loaded he thought she rode the sea as easily as the gulls or as serenely as the swans he used to see on the river near his home. At her mooring, if the sun happened to be shining, her varnished timbers looked golden against the oily green of the water.

She was the boat he most wanted if ever he could go to sea, to be allowed to sail in and yet despite his admiration and despite the fact that he was welcome aboard every other boat in the harbour Andy had never set foot aboard the 'Silver Crest'. The reason was twofold. Firstly, due to the poor fishing season 'Silver Crest' had rarely been in harbour for more time than it took to unload and secondly Andy was afraid of skipper Jake and his rough voice. Ever since the day when he had been sitting on a fish box sketching the 'Silver Crest' on the back of a letter he had composed to his father and Jake had been angry with him Andy had kept his distance from the boat. On Jake's behalf it must be said he was exasperated by the complete disappearance of his crew at a time when he himself could not leave the boat and in need of some information he had espied Andy. Ignorant of Andy's affliction he had bellowed at him as he would have bellowed at any other boy who looked capable of delivering a message. Andy went to the edge of the pier.

'Away an' tell Bobby I'm wantin' him down here!' he commanded. 'You know Bobbie? The little fellow with red hair.'

Andy nodded.

'Aye, then get him for me. Quick as you can, boy.'

Gaymal children accepted that on the pier they were commanded to do things – never requested – and Andy ran to find Bobby but when the man saw it was the 'Silver Crest' Andy was pointing to he turned away. 'I know fine what he wants me for,' he told a crony,' and I'm not going. I'm supposed to be catching a train in half an hour and if Jake once gets a hold of me I might just as well wave it goodbye.'

Andy returned to the 'Silver Crest'.

'Well, did you find him?' Jake asked.

Andy nodded.

'Is he comin', then?'

Andy shook his head.

'Why isn't he comin'?'

Andy stared at Jake helplessly.

'What's wrong with you, boy? Have I got to dig for every bit of an answer from you like I'd dig flesh from a limpet? What did he say?' Jake was becoming more exacerbated. 'Are you wantin' a penny before you'll tell me what he said? Is that it?' Jake, used to the money conscious Gaymal children, dug into his pocket and tossed a shilling on to the pier. Andy looked at the coin but made no attempt to pick it up.

'What in the hell's the matter with you?' Jake demanded. 'Is it deaf, daft or dumb you are?' Andy turned and ran quickly from his contempt. Jake climbed on to the pier hoping to spot another likely messenger and the first two things he saw there were the shilling he had thrown and the sketch Andy had been making of the 'Silver Crest'. Jake pocketed the shilling and picking up the paper studied the drawing. It was nice, he thought. Fancy a stupid kid like that being able to draw as well as this. He turned the paper over and saw Andy's painstaking printing. ' "Dear Dad",' he read. ' "This is the boat I like best in the harbour. She is called 'Silver Crest' and I think she is beautiful".' Jake wished he had not been so rough with the boy and going back aboard he placed the paper carefully between the leaves of a magazine in the wheelhouse thinking that next time he saw Andy he would return it to him and at the same time tell him how good it was.

It was three weeks later when one of the crew came across the drawing and commented on it.

'Ach, I put it in there to give back to some kid that was on the pier doing it. I sent him to get Bobby for me that day you lot skinned off ashore. The kid came back without Bobby and with not a word as to why.' Jake's voice was scornful. 'Proper little gaper he was, just standin' there an' sayin' nothin'. I shouted at him he must be dumb or somethin'.'

'Did he have a dog with him? The one that used to belong to Joe?' asked one of the crew.

'Aye, I believe he did,' Jake admitted.

'Aye, then right enough he is dumb,' said the man and turned away from his skipper's stricken face.

Later Jake learned from the crew the reason for Andy's arrival in Gaymal; learned too how he and the Spuddy had chummed up together and how the boy looked after the dog even though he was not allowed to have him anywhere near the house. The story touched Jake and as he pondered it he resolved to try to make friends with the boy. To see if he could make some recompense for the hurt he had so unwittingly inflicted. Back in the wheelhouse he examined the drawing once more. 'I'll need to try an' get a hold of the young fellow an' give him back his picture,' he told the man at the wheel. 'But God knows when I'll manage it seein' he never comes near the boat since the day I turned on him.'

9

The opportunity came when they limped back into port with the seized engine and Andy, curiosity overcoming caution, was waiting on the edge of the pier anxious to find out what was wrong. When the crew had gone off to the pub and the engineer was about to leave Andy started to move away. Jake's voice hailed him and Andy looked back to where the skipper was standing but he did not pause until he saw Jake was holding out a paper. Reluctantly he turned and went slowly up to him.

'Did you do this?' Jake asked as gently as he could and when Andy replied with a faint nod he said: 'It's good. I like it.' He turned the paper over. 'I read this too,' he confessed. 'Is it true you think this is the nicest boat in the harbour?' Andy released a nervous smile. 'Aye, I think so too, boy,' Jake admitted, looking proudly along the length of the 'Silver Crest'. 'I think so too,' he repeated, and Andy heard the pride in his voice. 'Are you comin' aboard?' he invited. Andy's expression was eloquent. 'Come on, then, an' take a look over her.'

Eagerly Andy clambered aboard followed by the Spuddy.

'Hey!' Jake objected. 'I didn't invite that dog as well. Away you go!' The Spuddy looked questioningly at Andy before obeying the command. The next moment Andy was also ashore and standing beside the dog.

'What's all this?' Jake asked. 'I thought you were keen to see over her.' Andy put his hand on the Spuddy's head. 'Okay, Okay,' Jake yielded. 'He may as well come too.' Andy and the dog jumped back aboard and followed Jake enthusiastically into the wheelhouse, down into the hold, through to the engine room and finally into the fo'c'sle where Jake put on the kettle.

'You get mugs and rolls and butter and jam out of there,' he instructed, pointing to a locker. 'I daresay you won't say no to a bite to eat.' Andy did as he was told. He had never before eaten any sort of a meal aboard a boat and when Jake had made the tea and they sat on the lockers to eat and drink while the boat swayed to the tide Andy was blissfully happy. He had got over his fear of Jake and Jake was glad of having to entertain the boy and so shorten the hours he would otherwise have had to spend brooding over his misfortunes. All the same he was finding conversation solely by means of questions difficult to sustain and for much of the time they ate in silence. Jake noticed Andy giving the Spuddy a piece of every roll he took for himself and recalling what the crew had told him about the dog being a stray which Andy had befriended and which he was not allowed to take home to his aunt's house he wondered how much the boy fretted at having to leave the Spuddy at night.

'Does the Spuddy sleep in your room at home?' he probed.

Andy shook his head.

'In the kitchen? No? In the house at all? No? In a kennel outside, then?' Andy continued to shake his head. 'Hasn't he got a place to sleep then?' Jake saw Andy's eyes widen as if straining back the tears and he turned to fill the stove, making a clatter with the iron lid and the poker while wishing he hadn't asked questions to which he already knew the answers. But his only desire was to help the boy if he could.

Andy covered his eyes, anguished by the reminder of his problem. He tried pressing his hands very hard into his eyes but the tears seeped through. Jake saw them and sitting down on the locker close to the boy spoke without looking directly at him.

'I suppose you'd miss the Spuddy too much if I suggested he could be a sea dog?' he said.

Mystified, Andy looked up.

'Here on "Silver Crest",' Jake explained. 'Why not? Lots of dogs go on boats,' he went on. 'An' there's folks say once a dog gets used to the sea he never wants to come ashore. Not to live, anyway.'

Andy listened half dismayed and only half believing that Jake was serious. His eyes questioned, why?

'He'd have a good berth with me an' the crew,' Jake confided. 'They're not hard, the men, an' there's always plenty of gash food aboard. An' there'd be a cosy bunk for him down here with us in the fo'c'sle. But,' Jake gave Andy a doubtful glance, 'maybe you wouldn't like to be parted from him so much.'

Andy stared steadfastly at Jake for some moments before beginning to nod slowly. There had been talk at Aunt Sarah's about a new schoolmaster coming to Gaymal who was willing, even anxious to have Andy as a pupil and much as Andy yearned to go to school he was worried about what might happen to the Spuddy during school hours. Jake's suggestion was perfect – or almost perfect. Andy's heart plummeted as he thought how lonely he would be without his friend. But if the Spuddy had a home, he reasoned, a real home where he would feel safe and wanted all the time, wasn't that worth more than Andy could give him? Andy's nodding became vigorous and swallowing hard he reached out, took Jake's hand and placed it on the Spuddy's head.

'You'll be able to see plenty of him at weekends,' comforted Jake as Andy prepared to go ashore. As the Spuddy went to follow him Jake took hold of his collar. 'An' if your aunt and uncle have no objection you can come out with us whenever you get the chance,' he promised. On the pier Andy's arm lifted in a slow farewell and Jake, seeing his crumpled face, could think of nothing more comforting to say. He could only watch while Andy ran along the pier and up the road that led to his aunt's house without stopping to look round.

On board the 'Silver Crest' Jake and the Spuddy went back to the fo'c'sle where Jake, telling himself that he was an impulsive fool, took the dog's head in his two large hands and stared into the Spuddy's brown eyes. The Spuddy returned the stare. 'What do you think of me as your new skipper?' Jake asked. The Spuddy's tail swung ever so slightly. 'Well, whatever you think you're to see you don't forget the youngster. I've no wish to pinch his best friend.' The Spuddy's tail waved more decisively. Jake stood up.

'Come on then, I'd best let you see your quarters.' There were eight bunks in the fo'c'sle of the 'Silver Crest' where the skipper and crew slept. Jake cleared out one of the two unused bunks and finding a couple of spare blankets threw them in. 'That's your bunk, mate,' he told the dog. 'An' remember a man's bunk is a man's bunk – he swops with nobody and nobody swops with him. Try it for size now.' He snapped his fingers and the Spuddy jumped in to investigate.

'Right,' Jake resumed, 'there's three things you have to learn aboard this boat an' you'll have to learn them pretty quick because there's not goin' to be much spare time to teach you. Are you listenin'?' 'The Spuddy pricked his ears and fixed Jake with an intelligent stare. 'The first is,' expounded Jake, 'this is your home from now on. The second is, I'm your skipper from now on an' it's me you take your orders from, an' the third is, this is your bed from now on.' The Spuddy's tail thumped once against the blankets and the expression in his eyes as he regarded Jake was one of perfect comprehension.

10

When the pubs closed the crew returned to the 'Silver Crest'. 'What's he doin' aboard?' they asked, seeing the Spuddy.

'Ship's dog,' replied Jake laconically.

'Where's his kid, then?' asked the youngest crewman, recognizing the dog and when Jake gave a brief explanation they murmured small pretended grumbles about having a dog aboard and hoped he would not be responsible for another run of bad luck.

'Not him.' Jake spoke with conviction as he gave the Spuddy a rough stroking. 'He's goin' to be our mascot, you'll see.'

And as their mascot they came to regard him since on his first night at sea with them they ran into an enormous shoal of herring and came back gunwale deep with their load. The crew were jubilant with the knowledge that their run of ill-luck had ended.

'I told you he'd be our mascot,' Jake reminded them and the crew accepted his remark with such seriousness that the Spuddy, had he allowed it, would have become more of a ship's pet than a ship's dog.

'He's worth his weight in steak every week,' asserted the cook as if daring any of them to question the sudden increase in the butcher's bill.

The Spuddy took readily to life at sea and as he saw the catches of herring coming aboard the obvious excitement of the men infected him and he raced from stem to stern, from stern to stem, careful to keep out of everyone's way yet still making sure he was sharing in the activity. By the third night he was so anxious to join in that he grabbed at

75

the net ropes as the men were hauling and bracing himself pulled with every ounce of muscle in his body. .

'By God! We've got a dog an' a half,' the crew congratulated one another.

After the third successive night of good catches the 'Silver Crest' seemed to lose the shoal and on the fourth night again they searched in vain while the Spuddy spent his time running restlessly around the deck or sitting wistfully in the bow staring into the night-black water. He was repeating this performance the following night when Jake, in the wheelhouse, was surprised to hear him start to bark. Jake was puzzled. It was the first time since he had been aboard that the Spuddy had been heard to bark. Jake was even more puzzled when a few moments later the dog came aft and began scratching at the wheelhouse door. Jake liked to have the Spuddy's company when he was alone on deck and kicking open the door he waited for the dog to come in. Instead of joining him the Spuddy only pawed at him and whined.

'What is it, boy?' Jake asked. But the dog ran back to stand with his two front feet on the bow while he peered down into the water and his tail wagged ecstatically. Jake eased the throttle and immediately a head appeared at the fo'c'sle hatch. 'See what's botherin' him!' Jake shouted.

The youngest member of the crew came aft, pulling on an oilskin. 'What's wrong, skipper?'

'See what's botherin' the Spuddy,' Jake repeated. 'He's behavin' kind of queer, as if he can see or hear somethin'.' The man went forward and as he reached the bow the Spuddy's tail began to thrash even more ecstatically and again he started to bark. The young man knelt down beside him, concentrating his attention on the sea. The cook came aft to join Jake.

'What's excitin' the dog?' the cook asked.

'Damned if I know,' admitted Jake, and added uncertainly, 'You'd think he must be hearin' or seein' somethin' the way he's actin'.'

The man in the bow stood up and turning gave a wide negative sweep of his arms.

'He can't see anythin' seemingly,' said the cook.

Shouting to the Spuddy to be quiet Jake throttled the engine down to a murmur and handing over the wheel to the cook with the instruction to steer in a wide circle he went out on deck and listened and looked intently. A minute later he was back in the wheelhouse.

'Go an' tell them to stand by to shoot the nets,' he snapped. 'It's my belief that dog's tryin' to tell us there's herrin'.'

Flashing him an incredulous glance the cook rushed forward to pass the command. An hour later they were gloatingly hauling in their loaded nets while the Spuddy looked on with smug triumph. Afterwards down in the fo'c'sle the crew looked at one another in amazement and asked, 'How did he do it, d'you reckon? By smell or by sight or by hearin'?'

'It's enough that he did it,' the oldest crew member declared 'What we must wait an' see now is, can he do it again?'

The Spuddy not only did it again and again but he became such a reliable herring spotter that if he showed no interest in the area they were searching for fish they knew there was little likelihood of finding any there. In Gaymal when the stories got around the Spuddy, instead of being regarded as a stray, became a star and though there were some fishermen who at first refused to believe in the dog's ability to detect the presence of herring the 'Silver Crest's' consistently good catches were irrefutable evidence of his powers and it was not long before skipper Jake was pointing out to his crew how even the most sceptical of the fishermen tended when at sea to keep the 'Silver Crest' close company in the hope of sharing the Spuddy's largesse.

When Andy heard of the Spuddy's faculty for herring spotting he was both thrilled and proud to know that he was his friend for though Andy was attending school now, on Saturday mornings he was always waiting at the pier for the 'Silver Crest' to come in so that he could greet the Spuddy and take him for the long hill walks Jake said the dog needed after the week at sea. In the evenings when the time came for him to return to his aunt's house Andy liked, before giving the Spuddy a special farewell fussing, to accompany him aboard the boat and watch him eat one of the meals the cook had left for him. When the Spuddy had become a sea dog he had to get used to taking his meals in the evening the same as the crew and when at weekends he was left in charge of the boat the cook always put two bowls of food out for him – one at each end of the galley – explaining to the dog that one was to be eaten on the Saturday night and the other on the Sunday night. To test his theory that the Spuddy was intelligent enough to understand and obey the cook came down to the boat on the first Sunday morning and found to his satisfaction that only one of the meals had been eaten; the other was untouched. When he came down later that evening again to test his theory he found the second meal had been eaten. For three successive weekends the cook visited the boat, not always at the same times, and invariably he found that the Spuddy did not touch the second bowl of food until the Sunday evening.

A year passed and the Spuddy became a cherished and indispensable member of the crew of the 'Silver Crest'. In addition to herring spotting he had resumed his war with the gulls, protecting the herring at unloading time as fiercely as he had at one time protected the fish for which Joe had been responsible. At weekends he guarded the boat like a sentry so that crews from other boats moored outside the 'Silver Crest' were heard to complain that though the

Spuddy allowed them to cross his boat in daylight when returning drunk at night they had to 'give the password like bloody soldiers before he'd let you cross.'

On board he could be trusted to keep out of the way of the crew's feet when they were busy on deck and except for falling overboard one pitch black night into a heaving sea while the skipper and crew were all too busy hauling to notice his disappearance he did nothing that would cause them concern. That night the Spuddy had been really frightened but sensibly he had fought the sea to swim round the boat to the side where the nets were being hauled and gripping the footrope of the net with teeth and legs he clung on. It was not until the incredulous crew saw him being hauled in with the net that they realised he must have fallen overboard and how near they must have been to losing him. Jake's fear had erupted into a flash of anger and he swore at the Spuddy vehemently, ordering him down to the fo'c'sle but afterwards when things had quietened down Jake laughed to himself, thinking he had never seen the dignified Spuddy look so utterly ridiculous and dejected as he had when he was being hauled aboard along with a load of herring. Jake called the dog back to the wheelhouse to give him a teasing and patting but following that night he always made sure the Spuddy was shut safely in the fo'c'sle when they were actually fishing and he never dared tell Andy of the incident.

There was no doubt the 'Silver Crest' became a happier boat after the Spuddy had become its mascot. The crew liked him to be there because it made the boat seem more homely. Jake was glad of his companionship in the wheelhouse during the long hours alone on deck; glad too of the dog's apparent need of him for though Jake knew there wasn't a skipper in the port who wouldn't be glad to offer the Spuddy 'bunk and bait' he felt that the dog, having accepted him as his skipper, would feel betrayed if Jake

79

were to desert him now. As for the Spuddy, he now had what he had always wanted: a home and a man on whom he could at last bestow the loyalty and love which he had not previously cared to give. He was in no danger of forgetting Andy but his feeling for him was that of a staunch friend; a loved companion and a playmate. But his skipper was his skipper and in the Spuddy's eyes supreme. After the weekends Jake would come down to the boat on Monday mornings and step straight into the Spuddy's welcome and as Jake gave him the accustomed rough caress the dog's top lip would lift in an attempt at a smile and he would snort and paw at Jake until the skipper bent down to receive the approving lick behind the ear which the dignified Spuddy never bestowed on any of the crew.

11

Andy's father came home on leave three times that year and so reassuring was his son's appearance and his obvious enjoyment of life in Gaymal that he was able to return to his ship with a contented mind. Andy was indeed happy: he had affection: he had school which so far he had not learned to dislike and above all he had weekends with the Spuddy. Also during the summer holidays he had been lucky enough to make several short trips on the 'Silver Crest' but, though Jake had invited him more than once, he had not been lucky enough to go on one of her longer trips lasting four or five days. His first chance to go he had missed through being down with mumps; his second chance had come when he was in bed with measles and when the next school holiday came along it coincided with the annual laying-up of the boats for 'paint-up'. Andy grew despondent about ever achieving his ambition to go on what he thought of as a real fishing trip: one lasting long enough to necessitate his sleeping aboard and which would take him to strange ports where he could step ashore with the crew and perhaps be mistaken for one of them instead of always being recognized as 'Andy, the dummy you see around the pier.'

The following year, when the spring holiday was approaching Andy was elated to hear Jake say one Saturday morning: 'I believe you're gettin' a holiday from school next week. We're aimin' to land our catch at a different port so it'll be a kind of longish trip. See now you don't go takin' anythin' that will keep you to your bed an' I'll speak to your Uncle Ben about you comin' with us.'

Andy's response was a broad smile which cut itself off

as he remembered his father was due home on leave next week. But Andy was sure his father would understand. He wouldn't want him to miss his chance yet again, he told himself and anyway since his father's leaves always lasted at least three weeks there would be plenty of time for them to be together when he returned from his trip.

The spring holiday came with un-springlike wet and cold and sleet and when the 'Silver Crest' speared out to sea at first light on the Monday morning, Andy was glad to be able to share the shelter of the wheelhouse with Skipper Jake and the Spuddy. Inevitably, it being a Monday, the crew were suffering from sore heads and Jake, whose wife was again away from home, was miserably aware of his own hangover and of the pain stabbing at his stomach. Hunched over the wheel he scowled at the tossing sea as he steered for the thick, grey horizon. The cook came aft, ducking his head against the spray and sleet.

'Are you goin' to get your head down, skipper?' he asked, reaching for the wheel.

'Aye, I'll do that,' replied Jake. 'It's not much of a day so how about makin' for that Rhuna place of yours; seein' you're always tellin' us how sheltered it is in this wind? We could maybe lie to in the bay for a whiley until we see what the weather's goin' to do.'

'Aye, aye, skipper,' agreed the cook.

Jake spoke to Andy. 'You'd best get some kip yourself boy while you can,' he instructed. 'If we're fishin' tonight you'll not get a chance.' Obediently Andy went to his bunk where he lay listening to the heavy thump of the boat into the seas; the scrunch of the waves and the smacking of spray on the deck. Thump, scrunch, smack; thump, scrunch, smack. The rhythm was like a cradle-song.

Andy woke to the noise of the chain rattling through the fairlead as the 'Silver Crest' dropped anchor in Rhuna bay. He slid quickly out of his bunk and went on deck to stand shivering in the first bite of the wind. Rhuna bay, hugged by two arms of jagged land was relatively quiet though the waves were fussing and hissing around the black rocks and the wind in the boat's rigging had a high-pitched note of menace. Andy could see the low, grey stone croft houses set close to the shore and beyond them, where the land rose to meet the hills, he discerned drifts of brown and black cattle grazing on the tawny grass. Skipper Jake who had been up on deck to supervise the anchoring paused to glare at the livid sky above the plump grey clouds that sagged over the hill peaks before returning to the fo'c'sle where, his face taut with pain, he threw himself into his bunk. Andy, aware of his own sea appetite, joined the rest of the crew in a meal of bacon, eggs and sausages along with hot dark tea, thickened with condensed milk and sipped from pint size enamelled mugs. Just as they were finishing the meal they heard a boat scrape alongside and the youngest crew member went up to investigate. He returned a few minutes later with two middle-aged men dressed in what Andy took to be their Sunday clothes. The cook was quick to recognize the men and when they had exchanged a few sentences in Gaelic he translated. 'They're sayin' there's a weddin' on here today. One of my relatives it's supposed to be too.'

There were questioning murmurs from the rest of the crew. 'Aye, an' they're after askin' us over an' take a wee dram with them an' maybe have a crack an' wish the bride an' groom good luck.' The cook's expression was eager. 'How about it boys? Just for an hour or two?'

It needed only a short discussion to reveal that all the crew liked the idea of going ashore for an hour and when they woke Jake to submit their plan to him he not only agreed but insisted they take Andy with them.

'You may as well take the Spuddy too, Andy,' Jake said, dragging himself out of his bunk to see them go. 'A run ashore won't harm him.' But surprisingly, when the time came for the Spuddy to jump down into the dinghy he refused to go. Even when Andy tried coaxing by patting the seat beside him and by pointing to the hills the Spuddy still did not yield. Andy noticed a slight quiver passing through the dog's body and immediately he stood up in the dinghy intent on climbing back aboard the 'Silver Crest'. The youngest crew member pulled him down again. 'You can come to the party instead of goin' for a walk, Andy. You'll fairly enjoy yourself,' he asserted. Andy still looked troubled but by now the dinghy was pushing off. The cook who had also noticed the Spuddy quivering called banteringly up to Jake: 'Ach, I believe the Spuddy's feelin' his age the same as the rest of us. The fishin' life's as hard on a dog as it is on a man. We all age quicker than we should.'

Jake gave the Spuddy a pat. 'Aye, we're all feelin' our age,' he responded with a sardonic smile. He was glad to be left alone for a little while. An hour's quiet and Jake was confident he'd be himself again. The anchor was good; the sea was quiet enough in the bay and even though the crew were ashore Jake trusted them to keep an eye open for anything going amiss. He went back to his bunk to collapse in a stupor of pain. The Spuddy having watched the dinghy reach the safety of the shore followed his skipper to the fo'c'sle and stretched himself out in his own bunk.

Jake was roused by the Spuddy's sharp, insistent barking. He was out of his bunk in a second. 'What the hell?' he asked himself, recognizing by the motion of the boat that something was wrong. 'The bloody anchor's dragged,' he muttered, consternated, and stumbled on deck to be met by a blinding blizzard that made him bend double as his eyes flinched shut. Close at hand he could hear the noise of breakers muffled by the snow but still far too loud. God!

She was almost ashore! He rushed to start the engine. Where in hell's name were the crew? Why hadn't they noticed the change in the weather, blast them! He'd trusted them, hadn't he? Fool that he was. Once the engine began to throb confidently his mind could grapple with the next problem. The anchor! Dismissing the possibility of trying to get it aboard himself he ran forward to cast off the anchor rope. That was a loss the crew could pay for, he thought grimly as he raced back to the wheelhouse and put the engine in gear. He tried to peer through the blizzard for a sign of the dinghy bringing out the crew but the snow was impenetrable, obliterating everything beyond the outline of the boat. Cautiously Jake began to dodge the 'Silver Crest' towards the entrance of the bay while cursing himself for being rash enough to allow all the crew to go ashore at the same time; for relying on the cook to pilot him through the narrow Rhuna passage. Where was that bloody cook? What was it he'd said to avoid? Remembered snatches of fo'c'sle talk rushed confusedly through his mind and Jake recalled with mounting panic something about there being a couple of rocks, submerged at high tide and well out beyond the coast to the west of the island. Just where were the rocks? And how far out must he steer to avoid them? He was shouting curses now; cursing himself, the cook and the snow. How near was he coming to the entrance of the bay? How soon could he risk turning? Gradually he became aware of a sharp lift to the sea and he heaved a sigh of relief knowing that he must be approaching open water. Resolving to turn westward rather than risk the hazardous passage between Rhuna and the mainland he headed the 'Silver Crest' directly into the seas, revving up the engine to combat the rapidly worsening conditions. Despite the cold his body was running with sweat; his hands, even his arms were shaking as he clutched the wheel and he found himself no longer shouting curses but murmuring prayer

87

after fervent prayer as the boat leaped and plunged.

The crash as she came down on the rocks flung Jake to the deck while the mast came smashing through the top of the wheelhouse. For a moment he lay sick and stunned, blood welling from a great gash on the side of his head and then he was desperately struggling to his feet to slam the engine into full astern. The propeller raced uselessly and as the sea tumbled away he saw that the 'Silver Crest' was caught amidships by two great fangs of rock that were holding her above the water like a priest holding up a sacrifice. Jake moaned. Why hadn't he gone out more before turning? How had he come to so badly misjudge his distance from the shore? The bloody snow! His stomach burned with pain and he clutched at it as he retched blood on to the deck. Staggering forward he clung on as another mountainous sea raced and reared to smash itself over the rocks and then all Jake was conscious of was the assault of the thundering water and the screams of his boat as she keeled over and the sea and the rocks began rending her apart. Gasping he lay on the tilting deck his hands gripping the capping while the realisation that his boat was doomed soaked into his brain as pitilessly as the chill sea soaked into his weakening body. He glimpsed the rocks again spiking through the snarling water; grasping, greedy rocks. Jake's breath came in sobbing coughs. They'd got his boat and now they wanted him. Those rocks, they wanted him all right. The thought hammered itself repetitively into his brain and he thought of his wife who didn't want him and of his infant son who didn't need him. Suddenly he remembered the Spuddy. Where was he? Could he still be down in the fo'c'sle'? Gulping and gasping Jake pulled himself along hanging on to the fallen mast only to find that the seas were breaking through the fo'c'sle hatch. The Spuddy must have got out, Jake reasoned. Was he even now swimming for the shore?

Jake hoped so but even as the hope entered his mind he saw the Spuddy.

When the mast had fallen the dog must have come up from the fo'c'sle and been trying to reach him in the wheelhouse and he lay now his hind-quarters pinned down by the wreckage. The Spuddy's mouth was open and he might have been howling though Jake could hear nothing above the savagery of the sea. 'All right, Spuddy!' he panted. Slithering and clawing his way along the deck he at last managed to insert his shoulder under the mast and heaved with all his remaining strength. Weak as he was the effort was enough to release the Spuddy and the next sea did the rest, washing the dog into the water. Relieved, Jake saw that he could still swim. The Spuddy might stand a chance of getting ashore alive. A dog's chance. No more. In the next instant he perceived the Spuddy was trying to turn to swim back to him.

'No, Spuddy! No!' Jake's voice came out in a rasping shout. 'Ashore Spuddy! Ashore! Skipper's orders!' Through a thinning swirl of snow Jake thought he caught a glimpse of land. He retched again and slowly his hands released their grip of the boat.

12

Back in Rhuna the crew, caught up in the jollity of the wedding, failed to notice the passing of the time and the threatening storm. Even Andy was too entranced by the old fiddler's playing to give a thought about getting back to the Spuddy. He had seen the sky darken and a few snowflakes whirling about but the house in which they were being entertained was tucked in behind the hill out of sight of the sea so it was not until they judged the time had come for them to return to the boat and they had rounded the shoulder of the hill that they became aware of the full force of the blizzard. When they reached the shore they were concerned to find that the sea was breaking so viciously over the shingle it was impossible to launch the dinghy. Andy could not hide his anxiety but the crew, feeling guilty over their inattention to the weather, tried to reassure themselves that there was nothing to worry about. When the tide ebbed there'd be a chance to launch the dinghy, they consoled themselves. And this blizzard couldn't last long, surely: not coming down as thickly as it was. They accepted the hospitality of a cottage near the shore where they drank tea and smoked and bit their fingernails and stared as though hypnotized at the snow masked windows. From his corner beside the fire Andy watched, feeling their unspoken apprehension. It was almost dark before the blizzard ceased and the sea was calm enough for them to get out in the dinghy and by that time there was no 'Silver Crest' in the bay.

'She must have started draggin' her anchor an' so he thought he'd best get out of it,' suggested the youngest member of the crew.

'I daresay that's the way of it,' agreed the cook expressionlessly.

'In that case he'll soon be back to pick us up,' said the oldest and they clustered around the dinghy, kicking at the shingle, stamping their cold feet; flapping their arms; smoking; muttering; exclaiming and all the time staring out across the bay willing the lights of the 'Silver Crest' to appear round the point. The wind died to a frosty calm and a full moon rose, polishing the dark rocks against the snowy collar of the bay and still the men waited on the shore, refusing the proffered warmth of the cottage. When the dawn came and there was still no sign of the boat the crew and some of the crofters walked out to the point to scan the sea. What they saw impaled on the jagged rocks sent some of them to summon help while others hurried to search the rocky shores.

When the sea had flung the Spuddy on the sandy inlet between the rocks on Rhuna's west coast it was the top of the tide and after dragging himself out of reach of the water he lay quite still. All through the night, oblivious of the thrashing surf, the cold and the pain of his crushed body he waited for the peace he knew would not be long in coming. When dawn came, lifting his head as if for one last look, he saw lying just above the now calm water the body of his skipper. He tried to move, digging his paws into the sand and laboriously, shuddering every now and then with pain, he dragged himself down until he was lying beside Jake. As he nuzzled under the cold hand that had given him so many rough caresses his tail lifted and dropped once and his breath came out in a last long moan.

Man and dog were still lying together when the search party found them. Gently they moved the body of the Spuddy aside while they lifted Jake on to a makeshift stretcher and carried him away. When they had gone Andy, accompanied by his father who, having been greeted on

94

his arrival in Gaymal by news of the wreck, had hitched a lift on the first boat out to Rhuna, reached the place where the Spuddy lay. Andy's father let the boy go down to the shore alone and as he watched he saw Andy bend down and tenderly stroke the dog's wet body. He saw him go then to where the shattered bow of the 'Silver Crest' lay where it had been washed ashore; saw him run his hand down the curving stem as he might have run it along the neck of a favourite horse; saw him return to the Spuddy and kneel beside him on the sand. He turned away then so as not to witness his son's grief and crouching behind a rock he gave his attention to the gulls as they circled low over the shore, listening to the laughter-like mutterings of a couple of black-backs; the loud harsh screams of the herring gulls until, thinking he heard a human shout he looked about him to see who might be coming. He stood up. The shout seemed to be coming from the direction of the shore but he knew there was only Andy down there. Andy and a dead dog. He looked more intently. The shout was unmistakably coming from the shore. 'No! No! No!' it was saying over and over again and as Andy, his son, was shaking his fists at the low swooping gulls his mouth was forming the word No! and the sound was without doubt coming from it. He stood in dazed unbelief while he watched Andy pull some string from his pocket, tie one end of it round a boulder and the other end round the Spuddy's neck. He saw him drag the dog down and into the water and fearful of what might happen he started bounding down to the shore calling 'Andy! Andy!' But Andy paid no attention. He knew he had to do this last service for his friend. He couldn't let the enemy gulls raven the poor dead body that could no longer defend itself. He must get the Spuddy out to deep-water; deep enough to be out of the way of the gulls and where the boulder would ensure his being carried out to sea by the next tide. As his father splashed through the

95

water to his side Andy let go the boulder and the Spuddy.
He grasped the hand his father was holding out to him.

'Andy!' rejoiced his father as they waded ashore. 'You
spoke. Did you know?'

Andy's hand went to his throat. 'No!' he said but he was
not answering his father's question he was still shouting at
the gulls.

'But you spoke again then. You really did,' his father
insisted.

'Yes,' said Andy experimentally and feeling the strange
throbbing that had begun in his throat he said 'Yes' and
'No', 'Yes' and 'No', over and over again as together he and
his father climbed out of the bay and tramped back across
the snowy moors.